AMERICAN
Legends & Tall Tales

Steven James Petruccio

Dover Publications, Inc.
Mineola, New York

Legends and tall tales are amazing stories that are sometimes hard to believe. It doesn't matter if these stories are true or not because we find them irresistible and entertaining. Some are historically accurate and have been passed down for years, such as George Washington cutting down his father's cherry tree, Sybil Ludington warning the colonial militia of enemies with her shouts, and Johnny Appleseed populating the west with apple trees. Others are highly exaggerated and contain characters with superhuman powers or traits like Big Mose who could lift street cars, Bess Call who pulled trees right out of the ground, and Old Stormalong who was thirty feet tall. For this coloring book we have selected twenty-two of these legendary characters to tell you about. So, take a look through the pages and enjoy reading as well as coloring!

Bibliographical Note

American Legends and Tall Tales is a new work, first published by
Dover Publications, Inc., in 2010.

International Standard Book Number

ISBN-13: 978-0-486-47786-2
ISBN-10: 0-486-47786-X

Manufactured in the United States by LSC Communications
47786X06   2020
www.doverpublications.com

BIG MOSE

Big Mose, also known as Moses Humphrey, was the biggest, bravest New York City firefighter that ever lived! He stood eight feet tall and could swim the Hudson River in just two strokes! Big Mose climbed burning ladders to save babies from tenement fires, and, having the strength of ten men, lifted streetcars out of the way of the fire wagons. One time a ship was drifting dangerously close to the rocky shore of the East River, so Big Mose lit one of his giant-sized cigars and blew a powerful puff of smoke at the ship's sails. That ship sailed clear down the river to safety.

DAVY CROCKETT

Davy Crockett, the "King of the Wild Frontier," was one of the greatest patriots of all time. One day when Davy was heading off to fight the redcoats, and riding down the Ohio River on the back of his pet alligator, a tornado suddenly came along. Davy held tightly onto the alligator's tail and grabbed onto a bolt of lightning. He finally landed near the bottom of Niagara Falls where the redcoats were waiting for him. They surrounded Davy, but he rode his alligator up the falls to safety. When Davy reached the top of the falls, he turned and shouted at the redcoats, "Uncle Sam and Crockett too!"

DANIEL BOONE

Daniel Boone was a hunter, frontiersman, and folk hero. He blazed the Wilderness Road across the Appalachian Mountains through Tennessee and Virginia. One time he actually fought off a big bear with his bare hands! Daniel was friendly with most Native Americans, but the Shawnees took the side of the British. He was captured by the Shawnees and made part of their tribe. While captured Daniel learned of a plot to attack the fort at Boonesborough. He made a daring escape and traveled one hundred and sixty miles on foot in just five days to warn the folks at the fort. Thanks to Daniel Boone the fort was saved.

SYBIL LUDINGTON

Sybil Ludington was only sixteen years old when she rode her way into history. On April 25, 1777 British troops were planning an attack. Sybil's father, Colonel Henry Ludington, was in charge of the local militia. When he learned about the attack he tried to send word to the local men, but they were too scattered. It was at nine o' clock that rainy night when Sybil rode out on her horse for forty miles, shouting a warning to all. Along the way she had to avoid the enemy troops and spies. Colonel Ludington's troops stopped the advancement of the troops and forced them back to their ships! Sybil became known as the "Female Paul Revere."

OLD STORMALONG

Captain Alfred Bulltop Stormalong was the greatest sailor ever! He was big and strong and stood thirty feet tall. Stormalong had an enormous ship built just for him with a mast that folded in half so it wouldn't hit the moon. The deck was so long that his crew had to ride horses to get from one end to the other. This ship called the *Courser*, could even outsail a steamship! When Stormalong's ship tried to pass through the English Channel it was such a tight fit that the crew coated the sides of the ship with soap so it could slip through. The ship was able to pass through and the soap combined with the scraping is what turned the Cliffs of Dover white—and they are still white today! Once he fought a giant sea monster and tied his legs up in knots. The creature eventually caught up with Old Stormalong, but the mighty captain forced the sea monster into a whirlpool and it was never seen again.

JOHN HENRY

John Henry was the strongest, most powerful steel driver who worked for the Chesapeake & Ohio Railroad. He spent his days drilling holes by driving steel spikes into the rock with his mighty hammer. John Henry could drill twelve feet each day and no one else could match him. One day, while drilling through Big Bend Mountain, a salesman came along claiming his steam-powered hammer could beat John Henry. Well, John pulled out two twenty pound hammers and they were off! The steam-powered hammer belched smoke and John slammed his hammers through the rock. Dust was flying everywhere! When they were done the steam engine had cut a nine-foot hole, but John Henry had carved two seven-foot holes! John Henry raised his hammers in victory. Suddenly, he toppled over with a thunderous thud. John Henry had died drilling his way to victory. Some say you can still hear the clang of his hammers in the tunnel.

MIKE FINK

Mike Fink, known as the "King of the Keelboaters," ran boats up and down the Ohio and Mississippi Rivers. He was described as half horse and half alligator because he was so big and fierce. He was quiet, but could snap into action in a heartbeat. One time there was a big alligator on the Mississippi River that was whipping up storms on the water with its long tail. Mike jumped into the river to wrestle the alligator. He managed to tie a rope around the alligator's tail and dragged him to shore where he tied him up so he couldn't bother anyone again. "He might be the biggest gator but I'm a red-hot snappin' turtle," Mike yelled out!

JOHNNY APPLESEED

John Chapman, also known as Johnny Appleseed, learned how to grow apple trees when he was very young. In fact, the apple orchard was his favorite place! When Johnny saw settlers moving west he knew they'd be needing apple trees, so he traveled to Ohio, Illinois, and Indiana to plant his seeds. Wherever he went he planted apple seeds! He wore used clothes and sometimes a tin pot on his head. Johnny was kind to people and animals and was welcomed wherever he went.

ANNIE OAKLEY

Phoebe Ann Mosey, better known as Annie Oakley, learned to hunt when she was only nine years old and became an expert shot. Word spread about how good she was as she entered shooting contests and won! She joined Buffalo Bill's Wild West show and displayed her skills using a pistol, rifle, and shotgun. Annie was only five feet tall and soon became known as the "Little Sure Shot." During the show she would hit a dime tossed in the air from ninety feet away or shoot six glass balls before any of them reached the ground! Annie became one of the very first female performing stars and proved that a woman could be just as good, or better, than a man.

PAUL BUNYAN

Paul Bunyan was the largest lumberjack of all time! He was born big. In fact, it took five storks to deliver him to his mamma and papa! One winter it was terribly cold and everything was blue, even the snow. Paul walked outside and found a baby ox lying in the snow, frozen. He took her inside and thawed her out, but she stayed blue! Paul named her Babe and they became best friends. As a lumberjack, Paul was so big and strong that he could cut down a whole acre of trees with one swing of his axe! In order to move all those trees, Paul would tie one end of the crooked road to a tree stump and the other end to Babe and have her pull the road until it was straight. Then Paul and his men rolled the logs down the road. He cleared lots of land so that people could build homes and towns all over the country!

CASEY JONES

John Luther "Casey" Jones was an engineer who worked for the Illinois Central Railroad. He was known for always being on time. Casey's train had a special whistle which started out long, rose higher, and then faded out. "There goes Casey Jones," people would say when they heard it. One April night, after Casey had finished his run with his train, the 384, he was asked to drive Ole 382 from Memphis to Canton. He agreed because he wanted to get the train there on time. It was a foggy night and the train left the station late. Casey was "highballing" his train at 75 miles per hour and made up the time! As he rounded a curve he saw a freight train stalled on the main track ahead of him. He yelled to his fireman to jump, but Casey stayed on board. He blew the whistle and slammed on the brakes. The train slowed down but plowed through four cars on the track. Casey had saved the passengers onboard his train but, sadly, didn't make it himself. When Casey was pulled from the wreck he was still holding the whistle cord and the brake.

SALLY ANN THUNDER ANN WHIRLWIND CROCKETT

Sally Ann Thunder Ann Whirlwind started talking the moment she was born. "I'm amazing!" she would say to her family. Sally Ann was pretty and she was tough, too. "I can do anything you can do," she would say to her nine brothers. Soon she became stronger and smarter than all of them. She could out wrestle the best wrestlers and out run the best runners. One day she came upon Davy Crockett who had gotten his head stuck in the crook of a hickory tree. Sally Ann made a chain out of rattlesnakes, tied them to a branch and pulled till Davy's head was free. They got married and had ten children. When Davy left for Washington, Sally Ann took charge of the family. One night a group of alligators surrounded the house. Sally Ann fought off every one of those alligators by herself. Sally Ann was truly amazing!

BESS CALL

Bess Call was strong just like her brother, Joe, who was the strongest man in the United States. She could pull a tree right out of the ground, roots and all! Bess loved to rearrange trees and boulders in the Adirondack Mountains just for fun. When it was time to do her chores on the farm she wasted no time. She would lift the cows off the ground to clean their stalls and pick up the horses to slap on new shoes. When it came to wrestling, no one could beat Bess! One man tried to, but Bess pinned him down and then tossed him and his horse over the fence. You don't get into a fight with Bess Call!

WINDWAGON SMITH

The mayor and business owners of Wichita were desperately try-
ing to think of a way to get people to come to their town. They needed a
quick way of transporting people and goods. One day they noticed a covered
wagon zooming its way down the road, surrounded by a cloud of dust. It was
Windwagon Smith! This wagon was special—it had a mast and sail on top of it! After Smith talked
to the mayor about the town's situation, he agreed to stay and help them build their own big wind-
powered wagon. They were convinced that this would save their town, as it could cut down on
travel time, making it easier for people to visit. The townspeople climbed on board for the first trip,
including the mayor's daughter. The wagon started out with Smith at the helm when suddenly a
tornado caught the sail and took up the wagon in one giant gust, never to be seen again. However,
some say if you look out across the prairies you can still see the wagon sailing across the horizon.

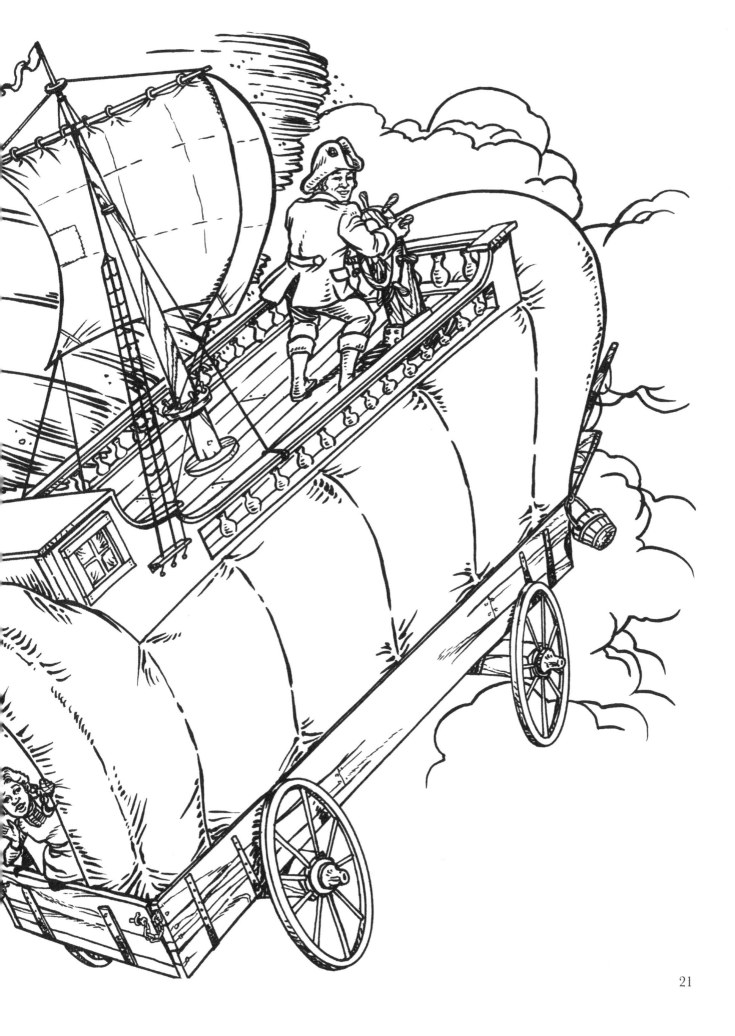

U.S. PRESIDENTS

Many stories have been told about U.S. Presidents which remain legendary. When **George Washington** was a young boy he received a small hatchet as a gift. He went about in the garden hacking at the sticks on which the peas grew. He saw a small cherry tree that his father was growing and chopped away at the bark and it died soon after. When his father saw the tree he asked, "Who has chopped my cherry tree?" After some thought, George said, " I cannot tell a lie, it was me that cut the cherry tree." George's father was happy that his son told the truth and from then on people trusted George.

Young **Abraham Lincoln,** when managing a country store, found that he had short-changed a customer by a few cents. He closed the store and walked many miles to return the money to the customer. Such deeds as this caused him to become known as "Honest Abe."

Teddy Roosevelt loved hunting and being outdoors. One day he was unsuccessful on a bear hunt, so his companions caught a small bear for him to shoot. "I can't shoot that bear. It can't defend itself," said Teddy. A cartoon soon appeared about the incident, which sparked the creation of a little stuffed bear cub, the "Teddy" bear.

MOLLY PITCHER

Mary (Molly) Ludwig Hays McCauley was the wife of Revolutionary soldier John Hays.
When she learned that her husband was going to fight the British in New Jersey, she

went to help. Her job was to carry water to the tired, thirsty soldiers at the Battle of Monmouth. "Molly, pitcher!" the soldiers would call out. When she saw her husband fall wounded in battle she ran to take his place at the cannon and began to load it and kept it firing. She stayed there for the rest of the battle. After the British retreated she was commended by General George Washington for her bravery.

SLUE FOOT SUE

Slue Foot Sue was the prettiest cowgirl you ever saw! One day Pecos Bill saw Sue riding down the Rio Grande on a catfish as big as a whale! She was holding on with only one hand and firing her six shooter with the other. Bill fell in love with her right there and they were soon married. Sue wanted to ride Bill's horse "Widow Maker," but Bill tried to talk her out of it because that horse always threw everyone off. Sue insisted and climbed on the horse's back. She was quickly thrown off, high up into the clouds. When she came down the hoop in her dress caused her to bounce back up and this went on for three days until Bill finally lassoed a tornado and went up and caught her.

BETSY ROSS

In 1776 General George Washington, along with three members of the Continental Congress, paid a visit to Betsy Ross. Betsy was a seamstress, skilled with the needle and thread. She had sewn ruffles and cuffs for the general before, so when a flag was needed for the new nation he went straight to Betsy. Washington showed her a small sketch of a flag with six-point stars but Betsy, being quick with her scissors, showed him how a five-point star could be cut quickly from a properly folded piece of cloth. They liked the idea and left Betsy to create the first flag for the United States of America.

PECOS BILL

Pecos Bill was an American cowboy who could shoot straighter and ride faster than anyone else! One day Pecos Bill and the other cowboys saw a tornado on the horizon. It was coming straight toward their cattle so the boys started herding them to shelter. Bill rode out to the tornado and rode it like a bronco. He grabbed a rattlesnake to use as a lasso and roped the spinning storm. He steered the tornado away from his friends across Colorado until the storm died out and Bill was forced to jump off. Along the way he carved out the Grand Canyon, and the rain created the Colorado River.

JOE MAGARAC

Joe Magarac was born in an ore mine, raised in a furnace and was made of pure steel! He stood seven feet tall and was as wide as the steel mill's huge doors. Joe could do the work of twenty-nine men and he worked all day, every day. Molten steel was poured into Joe's big hands and when he squeezed them together steel beams would leak out between his fingers. He was always there when the other workers were in trouble. When a bucket containing boiling liquid steel broke loose from a crane and was about to pour on the workers below, Joe jumped under it just in time. The burning liquid just poured down his back and the men were saved! Some folks say that Joe Magarac still lives in an abandoned steel mill just waiting to be called on again.